To my Leetie
Who has helped me
understand
The way of love.

♡

Momma

Other poetry books by Joan Walsh Anglund

A Cup of Sun
A Slice of Snow
Goodbye, Yesterday
Almost a Rainbow
Memories of the Heart
Circle of the Spirit
The Song of Love
Crocus in the Snow

The Way of Love

The Way
of
Love

Joan Walsh Anglund

Random House New York

Library of Congress Cataloging-in-Publication Data
Anglund, Joan Walsh.
The way of love / Joan Walsh Anglund.
p.   cm.
ISBN 0-679-41687-0
1. Spiritual life—Poetry.   I. Title.
PS3551.N47W3   1992
811'.54—dc20   92-53630

Manufactured in the United States of America
24689753
First Edition

WITH LOVE
FOR
MARIAN AND PAUL
KAREN AND PAM

The Way of Love

I have begun
                a Journey
. . . I cannot
                turn back.

I have begun
                a Journey
. . . and the Way
                        lies
                                ahead.

The Voice has spoken:
                Leave all things
                        and come with me!
                . . . I must follow
                                where
                                        It
                                        leads.

All things end

        . . . and all things continue.

All things change

        . . . and all things remain the same.

As I am Empty
    so
        am I filled.

As I become nothing
    so
        am I
            Everything.

  That
      which we have,
        is taken. . . .

  That
      which we lose,
        is found.

That which is valuable
                to one
        is useless
            to another.

That which is sacred
                to the holy man
        goes
            unnoticed
                    by the passerby.

Fame
　　　is a song
　　　　　upon the wind
　　　. . . and passes
　　　　　as quickly.

But Faith
　　　is
　　　a rock
　　　　　upon the hill,
　　unmoved
　　　　　and
　　　　　　　enduring.

It is in our Choice
                that all Power lies.

For that Idea
        to which we cling . . .
        becomes
                our center
        and creates
                a new world
                        around us.

And
      as the chosen seed
            becomes the awaited flower,
    the thought we treasure
      becomes
            our new reality.

Therefore,
        is it not
    through
                our differences
                        in viewpoint
        that
                we glimpse our Truth?

As
    the Mirror
            can only reflect
                the image given it

so
    the soul
            can only reflect
                the awareness
                    to which
                            it
                                has been
                                    brought.

The world's wealth
        is as the chaff
                in the wind.

It blows
    away
        . . . it does not stay

but the wealth
        of the Spirit
    is as the heavy grain
        which falls to Earth

        . . . bringing renewed Life
           to those who find
           and partake
                of its nourishment.

To be bound
         we have but
              to desire.

Only
         he is free
              who has relinquished All.

It is not with our Hands,
            that we shall hold,
but with our Hearts,

    and
        there,
                Love's eternal gift
                shall be safely
                        kept.

For Love has
    joined us all
        . . . it is but an illusion
            that we are separate.

Therefore:
    Be still
        . . . and listen.
    Rest
        . . . and do not strive.
      Be
          . . . and know
            that you are One
               . . . in Spirit.

Experience

      is a garment

           the soul wears

                . . . and discards.

Only that.

This daily Existence is but the outer apparel

      . . . it is not the living Soul within.

For all things

      seen

          with the Eye,

. . . all things heard

          with the Ear,

    all things felt

          or tasted,

              or touched

      . . . shall fade into nothingness,

    But the Soul is Eternal,

            and shall not fade

                but endure.

Love is not a Wall
              . . . it is a Bridge.
Love does not
          enclose
    . . . it opens a Way.

It leads . . .
      as a Pathway,
              winding,
    . . . to lands
              unknown
              and
              mysterious.

Let us follow
              where it leads
    for our Home
              lies just over the hill

    . . . and ever
              toward the Light!

There is
>   no
>   unimportant Love,
Each tenderness
>   carries its
>   >   unique and needed message.

Learn
>   from the Love you feel . . .
>   >   there is a reason
>   >   >   why you Love,

for
>   your Loving
>   >   points the way
>   >   >   to your Truth.

Follow your Happiness!
It is calling to you!
. . . leading you
to
the place
where you will find
your greatest
good.

For Joy
has purpose
as great
as her sterner sisters
of Reason
and
Duty.

Come to the temple
                of your Stillness
. . . leaving behind
                all distractions
        . . . releasing all desires
                . . . relinquishing all beliefs
                        . . . quieting
                                all questions.

In the Silence
        shall you find
                Your Answer.
In the Stillness
        shall you find
                Your Peace.

Who holds Love
        within his heart
        holds the Lamp of ten thousand flames,
    and the Light
            therein
                shall illumine
                    all the Days
                        of his
                            Existence
        . . . and beyond.

The wisdom
                of our Fathers
        is there
                for us to use.
It is a strength
                in times of trouble.

We do not
                dismantle the walls
                and roofs
                        that sheltered us
                        so long,

Nor
        should we dismantle
                the Faiths
                that have been our strength.

For,
        though worn and old,
                in times of storm
                they shall shelter us
                        again.

From the same Root
        grow many branches . . .
from the same Soil
        grow many vines.

Each Life grows
        from that
            which was before,
    altered
        in its way,
           . . . unique.

But
    the same Force
           flowing
               through each.

And
    the Way
        awaits you,
and the Journey
        now begins . . .

A hand
    is stretched
        to receive you,
A companion
        waits to guide you,
The path
    is stony
        but well-worn,
Your comrades
    are many
        and faithful.

Your joy
    shall be
        the joy
            of the
                Pilgrim
Who does not stay
        but travels
            ever onward
                toward the
                    Truth.

Be encouraged
          that you shall be
          of use,
For God's purpose
               is
          your purpose,
     and
          God's work
          will be done
               by
               your
                    Loving hands
                    and
                    heart.

It is not necessary
                to speak
        in order
                to have an effect.

To "be"
        is to radiate
                your being,
to have
        an influence,
        to change all things,
                because you "are."

Therefore,
        in Silence
        is the greatest work
                often accomplished.

        In our Stillness
                is Harmony
                begun.

As Peace
    is born
        in every heart
so shall it
    radiate out
   to join
        with all others,
until the Circle
       completes itself
   in
       one Universal Love.

We are "One"
       in truth.
          All separation is misconception
. . . a temporary blindness
           of the Soul.

But one day,
    we shall rise,
      one day,
        we shall know.
One day
    we shall recognize
       our Kinship
          of Spirit.

This is
    the journey
        of
        a thousand years
            at one Instant

This is the journey
            that, once begun,
        is never ended.

This is the journey
            of the Soul
      toward
            the discovery
                of itself.

This is the journey
        into Oneness
      with
        the Heart
            of
              God.

Let us hold
        in our hearts
        the sure knowledge
that
        past all tears . . .
            past all time . . .
                past Death itself . . .
        we shall meet again . . .
                        and
                            Embrace!

For Each of us
       there is
          a Way . . .
There is a pathway
       through the Darkness

   . . . a corridor
         through fear
   . . . a passageway
           out of sorrow
   . . . a stepping-stone
            across despair.

It is the Way of Love
    . . . of forgiveness
        . . . of tenderness
          and care.

It is the gentle Way
    . . . of the Heart.